CHAPTER *1*

DAV...   ...BROWN

HI...ON

HIGH MOON VOLUME 1 Published by DC Comics. Copyright © 2009 David Gallaher and Steve Ellis. All rights reserved. Originally published online at ZUDACOMICS.COM. All characters, their distinctive likenesses and related elements featured in this publication are trademarks of David Gallaher and Steve Ellis. Zuda Comics and the Zuda logo are trademarks of DC Comics. The stories, characters and incidents featured in this publication are entirely fictional. Visit ZUDACOMICS.COM for Zuda Comics submission information. DC Comics, 1700 Broadway, New York, NY 10019. A Warner Bros. Entertainment Company. Printed in Canada. First Printing. ISBN: 978-1-4012-2462-2

Ain't got to worry 'bout them no more.

'Cept for this fella.

PROCLAMATION

OF THE GOVERNOR OF TEXAS
WANTED FOR ROBBERY AND MURDER

EDDIE CONROY
MEMBER OF THE SULLIVAN GANG
REWARD OF $1000

Lawrence S. Ross

LAWRENCE S. ROSS – GOVERNOR

He came through here recently.

I'm looking for him.

Don't let the pretty picture fool ya...

I broke his face up.

This is a peaceful town. I *don't* take kindly to gunplay.

So, if you aren't a lawman, I *suggest* you leave.

Damn. You're that Pinkerton, aren't you?

Was. Name's Macgregor.

This town has problems.

This fella is the *worst* kinda problem.

Seems like you've come a long way for a reward.

Detective?

That's Fred Harper. Saw him leaving the Crabapple last night with some of the other miners.

When do they open?

Around suppertime, I reckon.

Plenty of time.

Time for what?

To burn all the bodies.

I don't know where you've come from...

But, you mark my words...

...come any closer and there'll be trouble.

Now, git!

Neee... ...huuup.

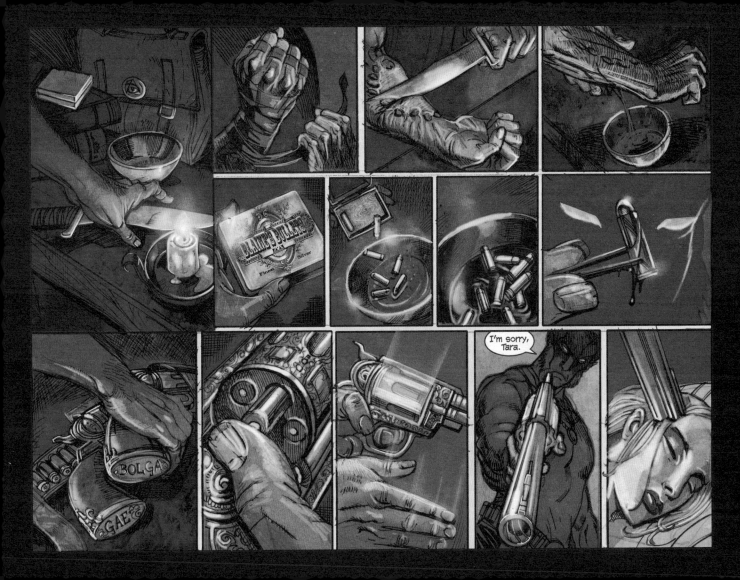

Sweet violets
This show is something else, isn't it, sir?
Sweeter than all the roses
Still... I figured this place would be packed.
Laden with fragrance
Pal, that just means more for me!
Sparkling with the dew
Sir?
Sweet violets
You feeling okay?
From mossy dell and rivulet...
You're looking a little...
AAAAAHHHH!!!
He's ours.

"This better be worth my time, Macgregor."

"It'll be worth a lot more than that."

Morning, little one.

Gotta get you some help, somehow.

Her family will be pleased...

They had considerable worry in their hearts.

I didn't mean no harm earlier.

No matter, she is safe now.

Found her a couple nights ago.

Tried to fix her up as best I could.

Monkshood kept her fever down?

Yeah.

It'll do wonders taming those instincts of yours.

Used the rest to fix up your mandible, I take it?

But, nevertheless, you did bring the Detective with you...

That changes things considerably.

HSSSGGHS

Guuuhh

Yeah... ...could've warned you 'bout that.

But I don't like you much.

HSSSGGHS

GRRAGH

SPKKH

HSSSGGHS

If I go, you're all coming with me.

You continue to deny yourself, Hound?

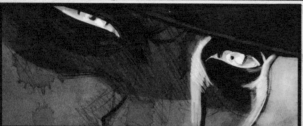

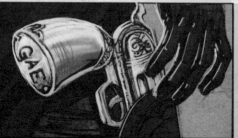

CHAPTER 2

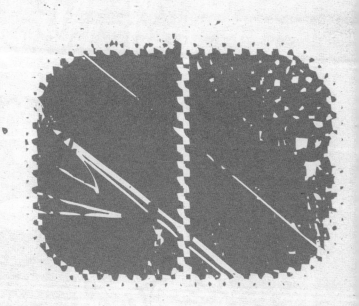

All aboard.

That's it. The Rainbow Special.

Sure it's the right train?

Hobble your lip. I mean what I say.

We'll stop by one of them Harvey Houses on the way?

I *do* like them Harvey Girls.

uhhhh... reservations?

All men *are* just as useless as you.

uhhhh... tickets, please?

Where's that little harlot of yours?

Guess they won't be seeing those Harvey Girls after all.

Last stop, folks!

No more snipsnap, boys.

This ain't what I'd call a bang-up job...

...despite evidence to the contrary.

How's we to know there'd be upstarts?

Or one of them Pinkertons fouling things up?

Hey, pa! I found something!

What the hell is it?

Doesn't matter much...

At least one of you can do something right.

Damn.

I found it. You can open it.

But I know exactly what I'm going to do with it.

Nah, Benny and I tried.

Yeah, it's too new-fangled for me.

This wagon show has a reputation to maintain.

And I had faith that you boys could keep the money coming in.

...but you are going to have to make it right somehow.

Sure thing, pa.

Yeah, what Andy said.

Lord, have mercy!

Quite enjoyed having you here, mister...

Macgregor.

Well, Mister Macgregor, how you fixed for lodgings?

'Cuz there's a place down the street that'll set you up nice.

Appreciate it.

Don't be a stranger.

Don't count on it.

GOLDEN APPLE

Ya gotta help me, man!!!

Please, ya gotta!

I... I...

There a problem here?

Something killed my boys...

..and now it's after me.

I'll settle this.

Got one chance to tell it to me straight.

I...swear... the truth is... just...well...

hmpf

My boys and I...*found*... something we could use for our show.

Didn't know it was alive...but it had eyes of brimstone and a fire in its belly.

They never stood a chance.

Take me to it.

Didn't you hear me...it'll kill me, too!

Somebody needs to stop this thing if'n it ain't done killin'.

Guess I'm that somebody.

"...and I have use for you boys."

Uhh...can I help you?

I'm the special envoy for Nikola Tesla.

That inventor back East?

Good evening, good sir.

Indubitably.

These are my papers.

But, of far greater personal importance...

I, Nikola Tesla, call to your attention to engagement work prepared to the specific grades of crime related to investigat detective work of all legitimate branches o property removed from the evening of Or Special on the evening of 1890. Associated ability, experie

...my name is Tristan Macgregor.

I'm looking for the man who killed my brother.

Because all I ever did was love you.

Lord knows it was never about that.

Your pride don't mean nothing to me.

But it's certainly got you all fired up.

And I don't know what scares me more...

...your temper...

"...or your brother's charms."

August?

Is that you?

Good Lord.

I cannot say that this is what I had in mind...

...but it ought to do.

Yes, it ought to do nicely.

Hello, gentlemen.

How fairs the young lady?

We got her stable.

But she needs the care only a doctor can provide.

Which means--

Our best hope is two towns over.

How disconcerting.

And what of your Macgregor?

It's raising hell from the heavens.

And this ain't the place to be.

Thank you, August.

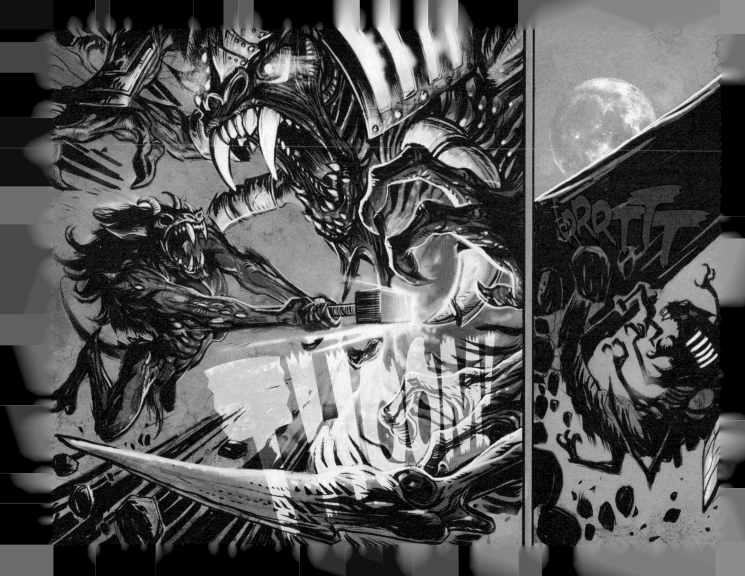

And I'm disappointed at your involvement, mother.

All my life I prayed for the spirits to protect you boys from the world's evil ways.

I made everyone suffer the moment Conroy walked into town.

Was too blind to grant forgiveness, when it was asked of me.

I'm sorry I got you involved in my ways, August.

Didn't know helping you carve those things would lead to this.

It makes you no better than him.

I know.

And your forgiveness don't matter much now that he's dead.

Actually, this might be mere conjecture on my part...

...but I don't think we've seen the last of this...Conroy Macgregor.

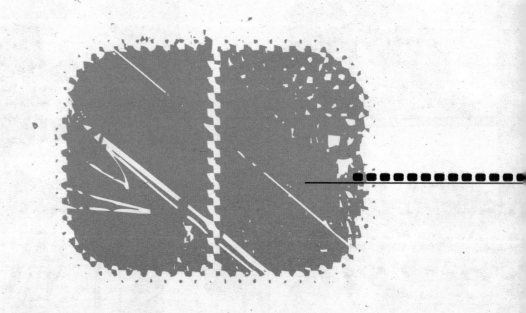

CHAPTER 3

GRRRR

Send my regards to your maker!

Tally-Ho!

Hello, Tristan.

Deirdre?

I've missed you.

ugh

Fergus, Tristan is down.

Protect Raven.

Raven?

These last few months were supposed to be scouting expeditions.

And I wanted to understand the Ghost Dance as much as anyone....

But how can we learn anything if you kill everything in your path?

This isn't the first time your tactics have caused problems.

The only problem I see right now, Deirdre...

...is that your husband is one of our prisoners...

...which makes both your allegiance and your usefulness rather dubious.

My husband is of no concern to me.

But he is to me.

On my mark, boys!

Now!

Time to up stakes.

What now, precisely?

We find Young Raven...

...before Prescott does.

You weren't supposed to get yourself shot up.

Not now.

You've made a fine mess of things, boy.

Such deplorable behavior couldn't go...

No.

It couldn't.

...unpunished.

Raven? I've been meaning to speak to you.

Appreciate your help saving the villagers.

That should have been my priority.

Instead, I got wrapped up in Prescott and...

It's just...I'm not much of a champion.

You will be.

● DAVID GALLAHER Writer

Named "Breakout Creator of 2008" by Comic Foundry Magazine, David Gallaher was the winner of the very first Zuda Comics competition with his high-energy, deeply researched, fusion horror/western webcomic HIGH MOON. In addition to his work for Zuda, David has written *Johnny Dollar* and *Vampire: The Masquerade* for Moonstone Books and *More Fund Comics* for Sky-Dog Press.

● STEVE ELLIS Artist

Steve Ellis's lush and detailed work has been featured across a wide spectrum of science fiction and fantasy books, video games, trading cards, magazines and, of course, comic books. At various points in his professional career, Steve provided artwork for LOBO, HAWKMAN, GREEN LANTERN, *Iron Man*, *Spider-Woman* and other series before dedicating himself fully to HIGH MOON for Zuda Comics.

● SCOTT O. BROWN Letterer

As a "Man of Comics," Scott O. Brown has been a writer, editor, and production artist for a wide range of comic properties. He has written *Nightfall* and *Atlantis Rising* for Platinum Studios and *They Do Not Die* for Ambrosia Publishing.

CREATORS

What are Zuda Comics?

Zuda Comics are webcomics!
Created by you. Chosen by you.

zudacomics.com

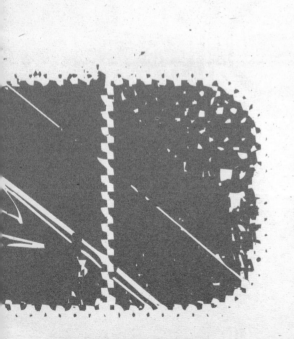

NIGHT OWLS By Peter Timony + Bobby Timony

A pair of detectives (and a gargoyle)
solve supernatural crimes in the 1920s
with their minds, mitts and moxie.
zudacomics.com/the_night_owls

I RULE THE NIGHT By Kevin Colden

Years after Night Devil died, his surviving
sidekick starts receiving messages from
beyond that reveal the disturbing truth
about his mentor.
zudacomics.com/i_rule_the_night

CELADORE By Caanan Grall

Two children are thrust into the
monster-slaying world of Celadore,
and it seems they would have it
no other way.
zudacomics.com/celadore

BAYOU By Jeremy Love

To save her father from a lynching,
Lee Wagstaff must enter a world
that is an eerie reflection of her own.
zudacomics.com/bayou

The
story
continues
at

zudacomics.com/high_moon